The Platypus

by Howard Zoldessy

ORANGE TABBY PUBLISHING

Knoxville, Tennessee, USA

Cover Art and design by Maria Loysa-Bel Nueve – de los Angeles

Paperback ISBN: 978-1-963281-05-7, 978-1-963281-06-4
Hardback ISBN: 978-1-963281-07-1, 978-1-963281-08-8

Printed in the United States of America.

The Platypus

The fourteen-year-old cornered his younger brother in the kitchen. Fearing another assault, the fleet footed eleven-year-old deked right and then cut left, escaping into the dining room, seeking the protection of a reliable barrier. Pivoting through two ninety-degree turns, the youngster positioned the rectangular dining table between himself and his attacker. The adolescent chased his younger brother around the table. Separated by four feet of polished mahogany, the taunting ensued. "You think you're so good looking, but you're not!" the older one sneered. "Girls don't like you. You're skinny and weak."

"I can work out and get stronger, but you'll always be ugly." The lad's retort enraged his brother. The acne-faced bully sprinted to his left, around the table. The younger boy darted through the living room, veered left in front of the guest closet, and bolted through the front door. Peering out from the screen door, the assailant watched his brother leap over the brick retaining wall onto the front lawn. Clad only in a flannel shirt, dungarees, and white cotton socks, the elusive prey whirled back. Behind the screen his brother leered and waved goodbye, then slowly closed the front door. The youngster deployed his counterpunch. "Platypus!" he yelled. The screen door flew open. The incensed fourteen-year-old stepped onto the brick landing, into the autumn chill. The boy repeated the slur, with more volume, "Platypus!" The attacker lurched forward but never left the landing. The boy ran off, wiping his eyes on his sleeve as he headed for the safety of his friend's house. Disclosing no true details to his friend or his friend's mom, he explained his shoeless attire with an impromptu comedic story. His friend's mom gave him a pair of dry socks. The boy returned home at six o'clock. His mother was back from her canasta game, and his father was changing out of his work clothes. As always, the boy would carry on as if this latest transgression never occurred.

When the younger son was three years old, he learned that incendiary insult from the neighborhood children. Once a week, he and his brother were required to accompany their mother on the two-block trek to the local ladies' shop. Returning home from that tedious outing, they nearly collided with a pack of ten-year-olds spilling onto the Bronx sidewalk from the corner candy store. One of the rowdy boys yelled, "Get out of our way, *platypus*!" The kids laughed and moved on.

"Just ignore them, Jamie," their mother said. Jamie was flirting with tears. The three-year-old was confused; he did not understand the incident and why his brother was weepy and red faced.

Two months after that disturbing encounter, the three-year-old and his grandfather were walking to the neighborhood's only attraction, the Bronx Zoo. His grandfather asked, "Do you want to see an amazing animal this afternoon? Let's go see the platypus."

"What is a platypus?" the child asked.

"A platypus is made up of parts that come from different animals. He wears a bill that he borrowed from a duck, a tail he stole from a beaver, and feet that fell off an otter. He's truly a strange looking creature."

In kindergarten, the young man received his first homework assignment. He brought a family photo to school for show and tell. The children sitting in the neighboring desks offered comments. Sammy, a black child said, "Hey! Your brother has the same hair as me. But I'm better looking."

Dorothy, whose family owned the German bakery, said his brother had eyes like the waiter in the Chinese restaurant and was as pale as the lady from Norway who taught them about the maypole. "He's not cute like you," she said.

Their words troubled the youngster. "Even if Jamie isn't good looking, he's still my brother." Now he understood why the neighborhood kids called his brother a platypus. Although he was younger and thin as a blade of grass, he would look out for his brother and protect him.

Years later, while working out the intricate details of a plan that took decades to formulate, the younger brother developed an appreciation for the inherent irony. The person he wanted to protect became the person from whom he needed protection.

The first assault took place when the younger son was nine years old. He was home alone with his brother. The day maid was off, their father was at work, and their mother was playing cards or bowling. The nine-year-old was in his bedroom, a small and remote dormer room in the far corner of the converted attic. He lived alone in the attic and enjoyed the seclusion. The attic was isolated and safe. The only access, an uncarpeted flight of stairs from the main floor, creaked and squeaked, alerting him to a visitor. The boy was sitting on his bedroom floor, constructing a village with his set of Lincoln Logs. His brother tiptoed up the stairs and barged into the boy's room. The younger son did not hear his brother climbing the stairs. "Dad wants me to tell you something." The older one leaped onto his younger brother. Using the bulk of his ninety-five pounds, he pinned his fifty pound brother to the floor, pressing his knees onto the lad's shoulders. The young boy squirmed and twisted his body. "You can't get out. Just do what I say!" The older son unzipped his fly and tried to force his penis into his brother's mouth. "Open your mouth! I said open your mouth!" The younger boy struggled and convulsed his body, violently moving his head side-to-side. The attacker rubbed his penis across his brother's face. The attack lasted ten minutes. The young boy was exhausted. He never unclenched his jaw. He never relented.

The nine-year-old had no recourse. His parents would disbelieve him and side with his brother. His tyrannical father could conceivably beat him for defaming his brother and fabricating such a horrendous story. In the solitude of his room, the nine-year-old dwelled on getting even. He was defenseless and powerless. Even the protective walls of his dormer room had been breached. He hoped that time would give him the tools. Until then, he would have to live with the situation—and be guarded and vigilant. He could not confront his brother, as that would inflame the predator and accelerate the attacks. He could not smash his brother with a baseball bat, as he would be charged with committing an unprovoked assault on his innocent brother, and that accusation would follow him for the rest of his life. The only approach, for now, was to act as if nothing happened and to conceal his desire for retaliation.

Several weeks after the first sexual assault, a live-in housemaid moved into the spare bedroom in the attic. After the daytime housekeeper quit, their narcissistic mother had demanded a live-in maid. The mother's daily itinerary of card games and clothes shopping left no time for housework. The mother had instructed the employment agency to send over a girl with an English accent. The second son watched from his dormer window as the new maid closed the cab door and walked up the steep driveway. She appeared misshapen. Her overcoat did not have a normal, uniform drape. One shoulder was lower than the other. He quietly descended the attic stairs and eavesdropped the conversation. The twenty-two-year-old female told the mother her name was Linda, she had just arrived from England, and the spinal surgery she had when she was a child stunted her growth. His mother ran through the list of daily chores, emphasizing proper telephone etiquette, and showed Linda her attic bedroom. Although the young man was embarrassed by the false perception of the family's economic platform (wealthy families employed live-in housekeepers and his family was not wealthy), he found Linda to be likeable and trustworthy. Linda taught him how to cook bacon and eggs, how to fold laundry, and how to play gin rummy. He didn't mind sharing the attic with her.

The second rape attempt occurred when the younger son was ten years old. On a cold Saturday night in December, he was watching television in the basement playroom. His parents were out, and Linda was up in her room. His thirteen-year-old brother grabbed him from behind, covered his mouth with his left hand, and ripped off his pajama bottoms with his right hand. The rapist then jumped onto the boy's back and tried to penetrate. The boy squirmed and wiggled around. The attacker pressed the victim's hands to the floor, the boy could not defend himself. The thirteen-year-old released his grip on one hand and punched the boy in the gut, then the boy started to cry. The boy kicked the leg of the TV stand and the television fell onto the floor. That ended the attack.

If their father had noticed the damage when he returned, there would have been a police line-up. Both boys would have been dragged out of bed and told to stand in their underwear against the white living room wall. The overhead lights and the table lamps would have been turned on and the lampshades pitched to illuminate the accused. Their father would have been gripping a thick brown leather belt, triple folded into a compressed weapon. He would have demanded a confession. The first-born son would have denied any involvement. He would have violated the obligation one has with himself to be honest. He would have sworn that he had been in his room all night, that he didn't hear anything, and that his wild younger brother was probably responsible. The wild one would have tried to fudge his way out of it. After processing the testimony, the father would have adjudicated. He would have told them that their punishment would be rendered in the morning, and they'd have all night to think about it. Then, he would have closed in. He would have stood over them. They would have smelled his seething anger and his cigarette breath. He would have feigned a strike. The boys would have flinched. In a low tone, the father would have snarled, "You disgust me. You don't deserve to live in this house. Now, get out of my sight." As he walked past his father, the younger son would have been kicked from behind. The discomfort and the black and blue bruise would have healed in about a week. The memory would have lingered.

Linda investigated the commotion. She came down from her room and helped Jamie repair the stand and lift the television back into place. She scrubbed and then polished the scuff mark from the vinyl floor. The lesser crime would be undetected and unpunished. The rapist believed the capital crime would evaporate into the ether. Disclosure was not his concern. The victim would have no credibility and, if necessary, Jamie could reverse the roles, he would become the victim of his brother's unholy accusations. Given that his brother transmitted no threat of retaliation and carried an ever-present fear of their father, Jamie believed he was invulnerable. Both sons had heard their father explain his parental philosophy on the nights he hosted poker games. "I want my boys to fear me. Fear grows into respect."

Jamie could not have fathomed the intense spiritual fire for revenge that burned within his brother.

A few months after the second attack, the younger son stumbled upon an unsettling incident between his brother and Linda. The young man had skipped his after-school Cub Scout meeting and come home early. He overheard Linda reprimand his brother; she told him she would tell his parents if he ever did that again.

Two weeks later, the younger son was in the basement searching for a wrench to adjust the seat bolts on his bike. He heard voices traveling through the air ducts. With the stealth of a feline, he crept up the stairs to the main level and heard Linda tearing into his brother. "I told you to never hide in my closet again! I'm going to tell your mum. Don't you touch me!" The younger son ran down the stairs to the lower level and pressed the button to activate the garage door, creating the impression that their father was pulling into the garage. Jamie retreated to his room. A few minutes later, the second son announced that he had accidentally hit the garage door button while hanging up his jacket. Linda packed her bags and left in the morning. She offered no explanation.

The parents subscribed to the ancestral custom of primogeniture; their first born son would receive the lion's share of the family's resources and inherit the bulk of the family's assets. When Jamie turned three, the indoctrination began, and he was told he would become a doctor. The parents wanted the bragging rights and the financial backstop. They would need Jamie's income to underwrite their golden years.

A botched diagnosis and a painful and sloppy surgical procedure heightened the attention the parents lavished upon their first born. In 1953, they ignored the warnings to sequester children during an outbreak of the mumps, and then they entrusted two coarse and somewhat dubious physicians to care for their afflicted son. The selective neck dissection to remove a swollen lymph node left a crude and jagged four-inch scar on the right side of Jamie's neck. The incision scarred the boy's psyche. The guilt-ridden, overprotective parents compensated, elevating the height of Jamie's pedestal. The second son begrudged his brother's privileges and preferential standing. He was appalled that a rapist was being groomed to be the family standard bearer. Jamie sensed his brother's discontent and enjoyed flaunting his status when the parents were absent or out of range.

The second son often withdrew to the shelter of his attic bedroom. He could not fight off his brother, he could not incur his father's wrath by seeking protection, and he could not upend the hierarchy by challenging his brother's status or his scar induced vulnerability. His eighty-square-foot bedroom was his only refuge from the anxiety. He fantasized about retribution. He would become the hunter. His brother would be the prey. Success would be two pronged, the desired outcome would be achieved, and there would be no trail of evidence. His payback would be so brilliantly planned and executed the platypus would have no clues connecting the violations he committed upon his younger brother with the ambush. At this moment, the second son ceased with the platypus allusions. That cute and innocent creature swimming in that metal tank in the Bronx Zoo did not deserve the comparison.

The second son believed he held a thread of leverage, and his brother Jamie might harbor a deep-seeded fear that his younger brother could ruin his reputation in the medical community. Only two people knew the depraved and vile truth: Jamie attempted to rape his brother. The younger brother was prepared to use that leverage indefinitely, until he had a plan for collecting the debt, even if it took decades.

Beware the rage festering in a patient man.

"Forget nothing, forgive less," the sixteen-year-old debt collector muttered to himself.

The second son was academically neglectful and performed below his capability. Although he possessed uncommon athletic skill, he did not sign up for any of the high school's sporting programs. He declined invitations and shied away from social functions. Seeking permission from his repressive parents was complicated. If their self-indulgent pursuits outside of the home conflicted with his request, the answer was no. If he asked them for a more reasonable curfew, again, the answer was no. He was not the equal of his classmates. They enjoyed life, liberty, and the pursuit of happiness. He characterized his home life as fear, insecurity, and the pursuit of escape.

In his senior year of high school, Jamie fulfilled a vital condition of his parental agreement; he was admitted into a university with a medical school. The parents insisted that their second son attend this same college, so their older son could keep an eye on the younger one. Only the second son recognized this paradoxical benefit—that he could keep his eye on Jamie. The second son scheduled an appointment with the dean of admissions at Jamie's college. On the strength of his grades he was not a candidate, but on the strength of his story and his personality, his academic shortcomings were waived. During the interview, he had noticed a cat in the family photo on the dean's desk. The dean had a sympathetic ear for a young man who had been donating part of his weekend pay to a feline adoption service in Harlem.

The brothers stayed in touch; maintaining his surveillance and that thread of leverage had become vital tools for the second son. On an autumn Friday in his senior year of college, the younger son drove home with a girl he had been dating. Before dropping her in Bridgeport, they stopped at his house to use the bathroom and grab a drink. His timing had been calculated. His parents were out, and his brother Jamie was volunteering at the hospital lab. Only the housekeeper would be home. The young lady said she did not need to use the bathroom and waited in the car.

Grabbing his laundry bag from behind the seat, he announced, "I'll be back in two minutes." On his return, clutching two cans of soda, he passed his brother on the front landing. There was no acknowledgement.

"Are you okay?" he asked his girlfriend as they backed out of the driveway. Her silence disturbed him.

Motoring north on the Merritt Parkway, she spoke. "Your brother told me he's going to be a doctor, and I'd have more fun with him than with you. He asked me for my number and told me not to say anything to you."

"I'm sorry he did that. I try to keep my family out of my private life."

"He looks nothing like you. I've seen gorgeous male models with those same ethnic features. But when the overall look lacks facial harmony, the features fight each other. Tell him I said he should grow a beard and hide that weak chin." Upon arriving at their destination, she instructed him to park in the street. She did not invite him into her home. She thanked him for the ride, closed the car door, and walked up the front path.

Six months after that incident, Jamie began to date a teacher who aspired to be a doctor's wife. The following year they were married. After the honeymoon, the second son observed another character flaw. His childhood abuser was financially irresponsible and naïve to the ways of business. Instead of preserving the nest egg of wedding cash, Jamie blew through the bundle. He immediately bought a new Corvette and one week later traded the Covette for a new Oldsmobile 442. Five days later, he traded the Olds for a new Pontiac GTO. Car salesmen salivated when Jamie walked into their showrooms. An easier mark they'd never find. Within two months, the newlywed exhausted the wedding gifts. The second son diagnosed his brother's behavior and spoke aloud to reinforce his conclusion. "He repeated the fatal mistake over and over again. He bought with his eyes."

When Jamie was a teenager, he spent a summer vacation at a co-ed sleep-away camp in upstate New York. A lass named Caitlin, a pretty brunette and the camp heartthrob, broke up with her boyfriend mid-summer. According to the gossip, the princess was on the prowl. At a camp social,

Jamie asked her to dance. "I think she'll dance with you," Caitlin sweetly responded, pointing to a homely, overweight girl sitting alone on a bench, munching popcorn and swigging soda. Thirty years upriver, Caitlin accepted the position of office manager at the same Miami medical practice where Jamie hung his foreign medical school diploma and his physician's license. He recognized her immediately. His cunning heart seized the opportunity to expunge decades of awkwardness and rejection.

Although the Hippocratic Oath requires physicians to uphold the highest ethical standards, the oath does not specifically cite trust. Neither Jamie's wife nor his partners could trust him. Caitlin and Jamie would rendezvous during lunch break at a local hotel, and sometimes they would meet in a remote exam room just to chat. Caitlin exploded when she found him romantically embracing a female patient in that same exam room. The eruption was widespread. Two marriages and the company policy of no fraternizing had been violated. Caitlin's husband filed for divorce and for custody of their two children. Jamie was asked to resign from the practice. He promised his wife it would never happen again, and she agreed to call off her divorce attorney provided they relocate to Atlanta. They rented out their Miami home and leased an apartment in the Atlanta suburb Sandy Springs. Jamie's termination agreement called for him to withdraw his funds from the pension program.

If fate selects our relatives, karma provides our justice. The second son's plan for retribution would now transition from the abstract to deployment. Over the years, the injured party had set aside capital to fund the project. His handwritten notes included a detailed budget of expenses, a script, banking arrangements, and legal maneuvers. He used untraceable mobile phones for executing all spoken communication. A voice-changing mouthpiece altered the tone and pitch of his conversation. All written business was conducted through various postal boxes that had been rented with a fictitious name.

Under that same fictitious name, and a cashier's check issued by a bank in the Cayman Islands, he opened a checking account in Atlanta and ordered one thousand checks. He established an agreement with an exotic car dealer and on behalf of a newly created shell corporation he executed a month-to-month lease for a corner office suite on the top floor of a twenty-four-story, class A office tower. The lease included two reserved spots in the attached garage. He issued the property management company a check bearing number 921. His remittance covered the security deposit, the first two months of rent, the plaque on the office suite door, and the lettering in the building directory. He correctly assumed that the maintenance man would be interested in a cash-friendly, after-hours side hustle. Following precise instructions, the dependable maintenance man arranged the office furniture, the monitors, the accessories including a decanter of Scotch and two tumblers, the décor, the stationery, the coffee maker, and the stocked mini-fridge. The maintenance man then mailed the keys to a designated post office box.

Staffing would be the final linchpin. To understand the underlying psychology, the justice seeker interviewed a Pinellas County jail inmate, a Ponzi swindler who had been chastised by the court as a moral degenerate. The interview confirmed the second son's theory; the enticement has to satisfy the narcissist's need for grandiosity and superiority.

Another insight manifested later that evening: a man's essence exists in his faults.

After several conversations and considerable due diligence, a defrocked SEC licensed trader living in Colorado Springs and a fashion model planning to move back to Rapid City and marry her sweetheart were added to the team. The SEC trader had explained that he had been set up and wrongfully punished and he needed the capital to complete the construction of his microbrewery. After a few rounds of negotiations, they agreed to terms; $25,000 with $5,000 up front, $1,000 in expenses, and maybe a bonus of $5,000 at the end. The trader also agreed to several coaching sessions.

In their final session, the trader asked, "Why are you doing this? I know you said never ask you any questions, and I don't know who you are or what you look like. But I'm assuming you have justification or you'd never go to this much trouble. If you don't want to respond, just hang up." The phone went silent.

That night, sitting alone on the pool deck of his four-bedroom home, sipping a tumbler of a peaty Scotch, the second son responded to the trader's query. "This will not eradicate the abuse, the bullying, the fear, or the anxiety. It will help me balance the scales. Lady Justice may be blind, but she carries a sword." Maintaining his anonymity was a twofold imperative. He can never be under suspicion, and Jamie can never have the opportunity to change the narrative and portray himself as the innocent victim of his brother's vindictive agenda.

Jamie and his wife settled into their Sandy Springs apartment. They renewed their passports and obtained Georgia driver's licenses. They ceased servicing the mortgage on their Miami home but continued to collect rent. One evening after dinner, Jamie answered the kitchen phone. A wealth manager introduced himself.

"How did you get my number?" Jamie asked.

"One of the physicians from your Miami practice suggested that I call and offer you a place in our fund. He said you were a damn good doc and you got a raw deal. I believe my office sent you my prospectus. I hope I'm not violating your privacy."

"Are you talking about the cardiologist, Neal?"

"I have nondisclosure fiduciary agreements with all of my clients. I'm sure you'll understand that I'm prohibited from mentioning his name. If this is a bad time I can call you back, or we could meet at my office."

"No, I'm okay. What kind of return are you offering? And what about liquidity?" Jamie asked.

"Fifteen to eighteen percent and twenty-four-hour liquidity, provided the banks are open."

"Eighteen percent? That's hard to believe."

"Come to my office. I'll show you stock accounting reports. I could show you a few client 1099-B forms with their names redacted. At today's close, the fund has $152 million dollars. I'm extremely selective. I only accept doctors, lawyers, judges, and CEOs. I work sixteen hours a day across exchanges all over the world, and I never hold a position. We get in and we get out. I never hold over a weekend or a holiday, and I seldom sleep with a stock. I'm happy to trade on an eighth of a point."

"How large was the fund when you started?" Jamie asked.

"Eighteen million. My personal contribution was four million. I've been doing this for fifteen years. I'd like to get out in five years, maybe six. My plan is to liquidate and distribute when the fund hits three hundred million."

"When will that happen?" Jamie asked.

"Based on current models and barring a catastrophic event, in five years the fund will have three hundred million. If we hold out for one more year, we can allocate earnings from the sixth year to satisfy tax consequences."

"What are your fees?"

"One quarter of a point paid annually. You'll see my compensation on your statement. I operate with full transparency, and I never comingle funds. My fees are separate, and every client has audit rights with no limitations."

"If I invest five hundred thousand, where will I be after five years?" Jamie asked.

"Five hundred thousand is a little light. I've maintained a minimum of one million." The wealth manager answered.

"Five hundred thousand is my limit. Can you make an exception?"

"I think so." The trader executed a quick calculation. "After five years, just over one million. If you hang in for six years, about one million one hundred and fifty thousand."

"How would you handle liquidation if I'm living overseas?" Jamie asked.

"That doesn't change anything. Several clients have multiple citizenships. Perhaps we should park your funds into a Swiss bank account when you liquidate. We can set that up."

"I'd like to look into this."

"We can meet formally in my office with our attorneys or informally for lunch or dinner," the fund manager replied.

"Let's meet in your office next Monday. I don't need to bring my attorney."

On Monday, Jamie drove to the wealth manager's office. The parking pass that was included in the packet that he received by courier activated the gate. He parked in the guest spot that was identified in the cover letter. A red Dino Ferrari, a rare and exquisite automobile, occupied the adjacent space. In the lobby, Jamie scanned the office directory and then rode the elevator to the twenty-fourth floor. An attractive receptionist greeted him as he entered the suite. As she directed him to a visitor's chair, he checked her hand for a wedding band. The outer office was adorned with monitors displaying financial data with stock and trading tickers flashing across every screen. Two centrally positioned, ceiling-mounted monitors featured market capitalization graphs and P/E ratios. "I think you're more stunning than this view of Atlanta," he said. She smiled and continued shuffling papers.

Jamie followed the receptionist into an oversized inner office. A tall fellow dressed in a blue, European cut suite and a white shirt open at the collar walked out from behind his L-shaped desk. Four large monitors arranged in a semi-circle would have blocked the gentleman trader from view. Rather than appear too obvious, Jamie did not qualify the fellow's shoes. He did notice the stainless steel Rolex Submariner on the fellow's left wrist.

After the perfunctory handshake and social platitudes, Jamie and the wealth manager sat on the leather chairs around the glass coffee table. A plastic model of a red Dino Ferrari was parked on the table. Moments later an audible ping sent the trader hustling back to his workstation. He stroked a keyboard and then he went silent and motionless. "Fantastic! We're out." Standing above the monitors he explained. "We bought sixty thousand shares at forty-two. We're out at forty-four. I think it's going to forty-six—and God bless them if it does. We held for three hours and took a one-hundred-and-twenty-thousand-dollar profit."

The receptionist knocked and entered. "I'm going to lunch. Can I get you two gents anything?"

"No, thank you," Jamie replied.

With his eyes magnetized to his monitors, the wealth manager responded. "I'll have my regular, turkey on rye, but please tell them no mayo. They put mayo on it yesterday."

Jamie witnessed another trade. With his left fist clenched in victory, the wealth manager announced, "We just cleared sixty-two grand. Now we're in four positions. We're not buying anything else today." The trader checked his Rolex. "Market closes in four hours. I'm worried about one deal. It's not moving, so I have to watch this one. Please don't think I'm being rude."

The frenetic pace, the luxurious suite, the Ferrari, and the Rolex sealed the deal. Jamie signed the wealth management agreement and handed the trader a personal check for five hundred thousand dollars. "If this were a cashier's check you'd be in the fund right now. I hope you don't mind, but I have to wait until the check clears. That's policy."

"Understood. My check should clear by Friday, but I'll call the bank and see what they can do" Jamie explained.

"Just let me know. I want your money working for you as soon as possible."

On Thursday, Jamie called the bank and confirmed that the check had cleared. On Friday, he drove to the wealth manager's office. He assumed that the parking pass would be invalid, he circled the building until he could find street parking. Jamie nodded hello to the security man, entered the elevator, and exited on the twenty fourth floor. The trader's suite was dark, and the door was locked. With an unsteady hand, Jamie summoned the elevator. His perspiration carried enzymes of panic. In the lobby he spoke with the security man. "Those folks cleared out last night. No one knows where they're at or how to reach them."

At four in the afternoon, an investigator from the Major Fraud Unit met with Jamie and his wife in their Sandy Springs apartment. The detective explained the process and mentioned the meager fifteen percent recovery rate. "Sounds like you got hit by a polished team," the detective said. Jamie balked when the investigator asked for the names and numbers of the people from his former Miami practice.

"Why do you need those?" Jamie asked.

"I have to start there. The scammer mentioned someone from the medical practice, and one of those folks might have a motive. They knew you left with half a million from your pension account."

"I don't want them to know. I don't want you to interview them." The complaint was dropped.

Twenty four hours after the deposit hit his Swiss bank account, the second son commenced with the allocation of funds. He never wavered, he did not seek reimbursement, he absorbed the fifty-eight-thousand-dollar expense for executing his methodical plan of justice. The trader and the model were compensated by checks issued from a Grand Cayman account. The maintenance man received a note to sell the office furniture to a liquidator and to keep the proceeds. The entire balance of the funds in the Swiss account, minus one thousand dollars, was divided equally into two blind trusts with Jamie's children named as beneficiaries. A fourth generation Tennessee law firm had been retained as the managing trustee. The law firm was under strict orders not to alert the beneficiaries for ten years and to immediately mail a one-thousand-dollar anonymous donation to a feline adoption service located in Harlem. The trustor, communicating through an overseas banking agent, was unknown.

Justice is both a journey and a destination. The second son did not fall prey to the passage of time that can wither motivation. He could not allow the crimes to go unpunished. There was no joy or celebration. There was no declared winner or loser. There were only degrees of loss.

He could not undo the abuse, nor could he quantify the fear. Time might tranquilize the pain, but time could never erase the crimes. The victim had done nothing to incite the violence, but he carried the scars and the burden. Navigating the mysteries of life while venturing into the unknown was enough of a challenge. He would never know how different his life would have been if his immoral brother had not attacked him. And now his attacker would contemplate that same unknown. For the rest of his days, his brother would wonder how different his life would have been if he had never written that check.

In spite of the whispers, Jamie and his wife circulated the story that they were retiring to a life abroad. Their immigration attorney produced a list of foreign governments with a limited extradition policy. In the lawyer's opinion, their sole means of support, the disability check Jamie's wife received every month, would be immune from seizure or garnishment if they established residency in one of the countries on the list. They broke the lease on their Sandy Springs apartment and left the United States. The tenant renting their Miami house received a notice of eviction on the same day the bank holding the mortgage filed a foreclosure lawsuit. Although the lender's attorney understood her extradition obstacles, she retained an international process servicing agent. Jamie tore the notice in half and tossed it into the trash.

"He's beyond our reach, and he's morally and financially bankrupt," the attorney told the banker. "Let's drop it."

Ten years hence, Jamie's children were shocked and elated to learn about the existence of the trusts, each account held half a million dollars. "Who did this for us?" they asked the trustee.

"We have been instructed to tell you this is a gift from a platypus."

Anonymity had been achieved, and there was no forensic trail. The second son's identity was safe. He existed in the shadows, surrounded by mirrors. No one ever knew his name.

About the Author

Sequestered in the hills of east Tennessee, this husband, dad, author, RE broker, and comedy historian has initiated a political movement to include moonshine into the ketogenic diet program. When not so engaged, he writes short stories.